Gettin' FIGGY

USA TODAY BESTSELLING AUTHOR
GAIL HARIS

gettin' figgy

USA TODAY BESTSELLING AUTHOR
GAIL HARIS

Copyright © 2023 by Gail Haris

All rights reserved.

No part of this book may be reproduced in any form or by any electronic or mechanical means, including information storage and retrieval systems, without written permission from the author, except for the use of brief quotations in a book review.

Cover Design: Yoly - https://www.cormarcovers.com/

Cover Photo: DepositPhotos

Man of the Month Series Managed by Kara Kendrick - https://karakendrick.com/

Editor: Brenda Mills Bastien

Chapter One

Rose

"Make sure you don't leave Tiny Tim alone outside at night. He gets so frightened and panics. Ebenezer will make a mess if he feels neglected. He's a sensitive soul." My mother doesn't realize how hard I'm trying not to roll my eyes at this nonsense. It has already taken everything in me to come to this wannabe generic Hallmark Christmas town and agree to keep her demon dogs, with the most absurd names, alive, now she's wanting me to baby them. She continues like I'm not about to turn around, get back in my car, and return to Tennessee.

For at least twenty years my parents talked about retiring in Candy Cane Key every time we came to visit. At first, I too was wrapped up in the small little

Christmas town in the Florida Keys. Until I became of age to realize how ridiculous it all was, and didn't want to spend a winter holiday somewhere hot. It had nothing to do with me coming of age where I could get my heart broken.

Every winter I would swoon over the dark haired Greek boy who worked at Niko's Taverna, Thanasis Diakos. He was everything I wasn't. Charming. Outgoing. Drop dead gorgeous. Soulless. Mindless. I look like I have a black heart, because I do. And it's his fault. I never wanted to put myself out there. He lured me out of my shell. As a shy child, I opened myself up to him. As a teen, I began to grow an attraction to him. Then, when I was eighteen, he made me feel… things. Only to turn around and humiliate me before breaking my heart and leaving me. I was eighteen, a legal adult, so after that, I vowed never to come to Candy Cane Keys again.

Until now.

It's been twelve years since I've been back. The only reason I'm here now is because my parents booked a cruise. They need someone to house sit while they're gone, but more importantly, tend to their pampered chihuahuas, Tiny Tim and Ebenezer.

"And we have a little treat bag for their best friend, Figs, for Sweetest Day."

"Figs?"

"The neighbor's dachshund. We do play dates every afternoon at three thirty. *Don't* miss it." When I stare at her with a blank face she elaborates. "It's part of their routine, Rose. I already feel horrible leaving them for so long. Please put your mother's mind and heart at ease knowing they'll still have their playdates, and be cared for. They're your baby siblings."

They're animals. But I know better than to say anything against the pampered pooches. These bug eyed little furry rodents get more affection than I, their *actual* child, did. I was loved, but I don't recall having regularly scheduled play dates. Maybe it's because they're retired now, and lonely. Who knows why they've taken an obsession to their little monsters on four legs. The idea of them going to a kennel, or coming to my house, was out of the question. Heaven forbid we disrupt their "routine" and "schedules."

Inhaling a deep breath, I struggle to maintain a calm and steady voice. "What is 'Sweetest Day'?"

"It's like Valentine's Day. But for friends."

I frown. "Isn't there already Galentine's Day?"

"This is different. And it's in October. You celebrate by doing something nice for someone, or getting them something sweet. Doesn't have to be anyone in particular. And our boys have a gift for their pal and neighbor, Figs. Don't worry. I also have everything written down and on post-its for you."

Do the boys have a gift for their big sister and sitter for Sweetest Days? Doubtful. *Oh my gosh I'm jealous of dogs.* I've reached a new low.

It takes my mother and father a solid fifteen minutes of smothering and fussing over my adopted fur siblings. They manage to pull all their strength together, and finish telling me goodbye, in five minutes. I watch their car pull out of the driveway and then disappear around the curve. When I turn around, two sets of big brown eyes are staring at me. I can't do this.

Grabbing my keys, I hop in my Jeep and leave in search of food.

"Naughty or Nice?" The overly enthusiastic hostess asks me. It's October. We're in the Florida Keys. Yet, Christmas is *everywhere* because this is Candy Kane Key. I swore I'd never be here again, yet here I am.

My parents fell in love in this town. They both happened to be vacationing here at the same time, and basically lived out a Hallmark movie romance. What happens when two Christmas enthusiasts fall in love? They have a child who is obsessed with Halloween. The only movie we all three loved to watch every year was *A Nightmare Before Christmas*. They made it a point for us to return yearly, and now they've retired here.

The music seems to be getting louder. Again, it's October. I get we are in a holiday themed town, but does it literally have to be *everywhere*. What's worse than Christmas music as the background music for your dining experience? Christmas karaoke is *much* much worse. I look to the right, or as they call it — the *nice* seating area. Families. Elderly. A very calm crowd. Turning my head to the left I scan the *naughty* section. Well, the bar is over there, so that's a plus. Unfortunately, karaoke is everywhere.

"Over there." I refuse to say "naughty." It's ridiculous.

"Ooh, on Santa's Naughty List, are we?" She follows that preposterous sentence with a childlike giggle.

"We are." I deadpan.

"Right this way."

I groan to myself as I sit down and hear two guys singing *Santa Claus is Comin' to Town*. One sounds like he's trying to imitate Elvis Presley, and the other one… well, his voice is really nice. That was until he did some weird baritone on the part about Santa knowing when you're awake and seeing when you're sleeping. I've always thought that song was ridiculously creeper, he seems to be proving my point.

My back is to the stage so at least I don't have to witness all this. But I'm still stuck hearing it. *Note to self, bring earplugs.* I wouldn't torture myself like this, but Niko's Taverna has the best food I've ever tasted. Enough for me to endure grown men making fools of themselves singing Christmas carols in October.

Chapter Two

Thanasis

My uncle Giannis, with his jet black hair and thick sideburns, wraps his arm around me as we harmonize *Santa Claus Is Comin' to Town*. This is a classic Christmas tune that I thoroughly enjoy having fun with. How can one not? Its creepy, and borderline terrifying lyrics sung to a happy and upbeat tune. *For goodness' sake.* I've always been a little confused by the American customs on Christmas. I'm Greek Orthodox, so of course I celebrate Christmas – I *love* the holiday. Everything about Christmas is freaking awesome. However, I spent my Christmases in Greece until I was nine. We got our presents on New Year's. Santa didn't come on Jesus's birthday, because he'd bring in the New Year. He'd come to town, and be in our village square. No big guy in red was breaking into houses at night and eating cookies. He wasn't creeping around checking on us. Ole Saint Nick didn't need to, my *yiayia* – grandmother – kept everyone in line with one look. She also kept us well-fed, and taught us everything we know about the passion of cooking. From the village of Greece to Candy Cane Key in Florida, we now blend both of our worlds. *Santa Claus Is Comin' To Town* is one of my karaoke go-to's simply for the humor I find in some of the lyrics, and I still remember Santa coming to our little village center.

White Christmas lights twinkle from the ceilings. Garlands made of fig leaves, and multicolored classic rounded bulb lights, are wrapped around the columns that are scattered throughout the restaurant. Our atmosphere is the perfect balance of holiday cheer and Mediterranean kick back vibes. Situated right on the beach, Niko's Taverna somehow manages to be a fun family restaurant and a party and hangout spot. The menu has a variety of Christmas traditional classics, along with our specialty – Greek cuisine. Homemade recipes passed down through the generations. But our main attraction is the *naughty or nice* seating, and Christmas karaoke.

The karaoke is a hit for all ages, mainly because *everyone* knows at least a few holiday songs. There's not a dry eye in the place when a little girl sings *Silent Night*. No sour face can be found when you hear a group of guys try to imitate the Platter's version of

White Christmas. And everyone loves when my uncle Giannis, a professional Elvis Presley tribute artist, sings his rendition of *Blue Christmas*. Tonight he is doing me the honor of making *Santa Claus Is Comin' To Town,* a duet.

The song ends and Giannis wraps me in a hug. "Bravo!"

"Thanks, Theo." Theo is the Greek word for uncle. "I better get back behind the bar."

I love bartending here. What nobody knows is, technically, I'm the owner. Niko's youngest son Alexi wanted to venture out and try somewhere new for a while. He isn't ready for any responsiblities. His other kids never wanted it, and he's in sixties. I'd always loved being here, and the restaurant business is in my blood. Two years ago I purchased it, but told him that he still runs the show as far as everyone else is concerned. Employees still report to me, and I'm the one to deal with all the bullshit that comes with dealing with people, but as far as anyone knows, I'm the *manager*. It's still Niko's Taverna. I'll never change the name because he was the one who traveled from Greece and risked it all to bring his vision to life. To most people, I'm not even known as the manager, but just the bartender Thanasis. I do it all. If we're short staffed on servers, I'm your waiter. Dishwasher or busboy couldn't make it in? Give me a scrubber and tub. I'll have the tables cleaned in seconds. Cook called in? Give me an apron and let's go. There's not a job I can't, or won't, do in the restaurant. But my favorite is bartending. I love people. I love mixing drinks, coming up with new ones, and interacting with locals as well as the tourists.

An older gentleman orders my special for this week, *Getting' Figgy*. I whip up the purple cocktail and then wait patiently as he tries it.

"I didn't think I'd like it, but it's actually pretty good."

"Never know until you try, right?" I tease as I clean up my station.

Currently singing *"Jingle Bell Rock,"* is a group of guys in their early twenties. They're

very animated as their large bodies awkwardly try to get in sync with their can-can dance and jazz hands. It's a great performance as the one on the end is providing a very deep, and heavy bass, on backup.

The guy speaks again, taking my attention away from the show, "What made you think figs?"

"Sweetest Day is a popular holiday between my neighbors and me So – "

"Sweetest Day? Is that some sort of made-up holiday?"

"No, it's real. It's more popular in the Midwest, but quite a few here in the Keys celebrate it. Think Valentine's Day, but not limited. You can use it to give sweets to express interest, or just as an act of kindness. You don't have to have a reason, everyone deserves something sweet on Sweetest Day."

"Sounds like another marketing scam for candy companies. Don't they already have Halloween to increase their sales? And Christmas. And Valentine's Day. And Easter."

"It's fun. Let's just go with that. I wanted to make a drink, and in Ancient Greece, fig trees would be bestowed on winners in competitions. Plus purple goes with Halloween, don't you think?"

"But we're a Christmas town."

"Yeah. Purple blends better than orange, don't you think? Figs are also great for Christmas. It's the perfect blend for either holiday. And especially great for Sweetest Day."

"Why *Gettin' Figgy* for the name?"

What is with this interrogation? It's a drink special. I force a smile. "Well, the fig is also romantic. It's a symbol of fertility."

The man stares at me for a while and then looks at the drink. The awkwardness is growing by the second. Finally he bursts out laughing. "And after a few drinks you'll feel like *getting figgy*, huh? I like you Thanasis. Good work, buddy."

He gives me a salute with his glass and then downs his drink before walking away. I watch him go to the door where he pauses to let a woman pass.

Was that… No. I shake my head and laugh to myself. I've waited for her to return to Candy Cane Key for years. Her parents, Mr. and Mrs. Verbeck, would've told me if she was coming to visit.

Wouldn't they?

Chapter Three

Rose

These dogs are not responding to me. I keep trying to call them so they'll go outside to do their business, but they stare at me. "You're going to make me say it, aren't you?" They tilt their little heads. I'll admit, the overgrown rodents are kind of cute. *Kind of.* Taking in a deep, calming breath and slowly blowing out of my mouth, I brace myself for how ridiculous I'm about to be. In a sweet voice that is typically reserved for babies, I say, "Come on Tiny. Come on. Come on Tiny.., Tim." They're little tails wag with excitement. That's a promising sign. Definitely more than I've been getting out of them. "Here Ebenezer. Let's go potty, Ebenezer."

The two pampered poochies bounce on the pads

of their little feet before hopping off the couch to come join me by the back door. They stop at my feet and look up at me expectantly. I read over my mother's note. *Please dress them appropriately. They don't like to go out without being properly dressed.* I turn to the array of little shirts, rompers, bowties, bling collars, and sweaters. It's too warm for a sweater, so we'll go with a checkered romper for Ebenezer and PAWSOME shirt and lime bowtie for Tiny Tim. Once we're dressed I read the next thing on her instructions. *Give Figs his gift for Sweetest Day, October 21st.* That's today. I grab the bag with a bow and "Figs" on the hanging tag. *Let's go meet Figs.*

It's weird being here again. The town is more touristy, but it still maintains the sweet small town vibe. I wonder if… Nope. Not going to think about Tha-nasty. Than-ass-is. I have so many names for that over-the-top Greek Casanova. Candy Cane Key isn't a very big place, but I think if I try really hard, I'll be able to avoid him.

"Tiny Tim! Ebenezer! Figs was about to break the door down to see you." A smooth, deep voice calls. Sounds younger than I was expecting. I assumed Mom's neighbor and puppy power enthusiasts would be older andretired like herself. With a smile plastered on my face, I spin around to see an overly hyper dachshund, wearing a tropical button up shirt with a popped collar, at the gate that connects our yard with a community play area. There, opening the gate, is… *Oh shit.*

He must feel the same way. When our eyes meet, his widen as he mouths, "Oh shit." But then his face transforms into a huge smile that reveals his perfectly straight white teeth. "So that was you!"

"Me?"

Thanasis opens the gate and allows Figs to rush up to lick the two diva chihuahuas. He strolls up to me in his steel grey slacks and purple button up. With those leg longs, it only takes him a few steps before we're standing toe to toe. "At Niko's. If my eyes didn't deceive me about seeing you, that must also mean you were exiting the *naughty* side."

I cross my arms and refuse to be baited by his charming good looks and seductive voice. "The naughty side was less crowded."

"Sure it was." I don't appreciate his mocking tone.

"I didn't realize you were still working there."

The corner of his lip twitches as he fights back a smirk. "I didn't realize you were in town."

"Not for long." Might be even shorter now. Neighbors with *him*, what were my parents thinking? They deserve this vacation, but this little oversight of detail has me tempted to call them and demand they return home, or the pups are relocating. When we continue to stand there staring at one another, I explain. "I'm house sitting."

"Tending to Tiny Tim and Ebenezer, too?"

"Yes. Now if you'll excuse me." I step around him and march away. Ebenezer is squatting and straining to relieve himself. My eyebrows pull together in concern. *Is it normal for him to tremble so much while pooping?*

A shadow looms over me as Thanasis comes to stand next to me. "Where's your bag?"

"My bag?" I force myself to sound bored and not like my heart is racing having him so close to me.

"To pick up their... droppings?" My eyes widen. He chuckles and hands me a blue bag. "Here. I have an extra."

Another couple follows their little pooch, and I watch as they use the bag and scoop up the feces. Then they look over at me. *See? That's how it's done.* Is what they seem to be telling me. I give a tight smile and jerk the bag from Thanasis. He follows me as I begin to walk so I pause, and still without looking at him, I say, "You don't have to go with me."

"Oh, but I do. Support." *Yeah, I bet.*

Ebenezer kicks his little feet in the opposite direction of his two mini logs. I sincerely hope he doesn't actually think he's burying it. He prances away like a show dog that won the blue ribbon. *This is gross.* No. It's no big deal. It's fine. At least it's small. I cover my hand with a part of the bag to use as a glove.

It's so warm... I'm fine. This is fine.

It smells horrendous. How does something so small produce such a foul odor? All is well. Just gotta drop this in here...

"Looks like the long Tootsie Rolls, huh?"

No he didn't. He did not just compare this turd in my hand to a Tootsie Roll.

"You know the candy?"

"Yes! Why would you ruin them for me?"

"I didn't say it would tas – "

"Please stop."

"The droppings bear a resemblance to a particular chocolate candy. That's all I'm saying."

The laughter in his eyes has me considering the idea of flinging the steamy little dropping at his shoe. But that'd be disgusting. I quickly dispose of it in the bag and tie it. "You maybe should've waited before tying it. Tiny Tim might leave some gifts as well."

"I need to go wash my hands. I'll get another bag. Do you mind watching them?"

"Are you going to forgive me for something that happened twelve years ago?" He seriously had to bring that up.

"Nope."

"You don't want to clear the air? Find some sort of closure?"

"Nope."

I begin walking and he follows. "But it's Sweetest Day. It's the perfect day to make up and restore our friendship. We used to be so close."

"The dogs. Shouldn't one of us be watching them? Like you."

He whistles and all three dogs waddle after us. "No worries. Now, let's talk. You never even gave me a chance to explain. You left and never came back. I wrote you letters."

"You did? I didn't read them."

"I know. Your parents told me."

"How much do you and my parents talk?"

"We're neighbors now, but they always came to the Taverna." *Of course they did.*

I stop and stare slack-jawed at him. "Was this their plan all along? Were you part of this plan? Did you know I'd be here?"

He laughs, and it only angers me more. *He's laughing at me… again.* "Don't be silly."

"Don't call me silly."

"Sorry. I didn't mean – " He pauses. Hopefully to gather his thoughts and think before he speaks again. "I don't know why I keep screwing this up. How about a deal?" His warm fingers gently touch my elbow to bring me to a stop. "I'll finish with these guys. And I'll take them out again before my shift tonight. In return, you come in tonight and try my signature drink *Gettin' Figgy*."

I suck my lips in and close my eyes. He would name it that. "What's your obsession with figs? Dog's name. Restaurant décor had fig leaves. You have a fig tree in your backyard. Now the drink."

"I've got a theme. But you come in and have one drink with me, I'll leave you alone for the rest of your time here."

"And what? Are you threatening to annoy me until my time is up if I don't? Plus," I poke his chest, "You first said to *try* the drink. Now it's *have* a drink with you. You've already changed the details of the deal."

Before Thanasis can answer, the dogs begin

barking and take off in a hard run. "No! No! I can't lose them!" I shout . I drop the bag on the ground and run after the three stylishly dressed miniature dogs. I finally see what they're chasing.

A chicken.

But why is there a chicken?

The chicken darts through a metal fence, and then looks through the gate at the three dogs who are barking like they're six feet tall.

"Figs! What have I told you about chasing, Honey?" Thanasis gives me an apologetic smile. "Sorry. I forgot about Honey. Sometimes they let her roam, and if these guys see her they can't resist the chase."

"Will they hurt her?"

"No, no, no. She's stopped before, and so do they. Figs here wouldn't know what to do with her if he did catch her."

I fight back a smile as I say, "Must've taken after you." Thanasis is a good sport about my burn and laughs it off. I bend down to pick up Tiny Tim, but the little dick has the nerve to growl at me. He remains focused on Honey, who is now flaunting her victory by clucking up and down along the fence.

"He's not going to bite," Thanasis assures me, but I see sharp little teeth. When I don't move, I can practically see the light bulb appear over his stupidly styled perfect hair. "I'll bring them back to the house… *if* you sit in a booth, and share one drink with me, tonight – *Gettin' Figgy*. One glass. And we have to sit together."

I try to pick up Ebenezer, and that little scrooge growls as well. Accepting this defeat, mainly because I could go for a drink tonight, "Fine."

With that, I turn and march back to the house, leaving Thanasis to deliver those spoiled little fur balls.

Chapter Four

Thanasis

My smile remains in place as I carry Tiny and Eb as Figs follows us. "You guys are going to have to go easy on Rose, aight?" They look up at me with their sweet big round eyes. "She'll warm up to you guys. It's me. I'm making her more tense about being here." Tiny gives my hand a little lick. "Thanks pal. I goofed, and embarrassed her, years ago. She still hasn't forgiven me."

I walk through the gate as I have so many times before. Rose left the door unlocked so I opened it enough for the two fur babies to get through. "Here we go guys."

Their little nails clack against the floor as they go to their personalized water bowls. There's no sign of

Rose, so I turn the lock on the door knob and shut the door. I don't want to risk her leaving the door unlocked. This is a safe neighborhood, but still.

Nerves have made me unable to sit still until my shift starts. Rose and I are going to finally speak after twelve years. We're going to share a drink. It's not a date… but she's setting aside time for me. I've never moved on from Rose. Sure, there've been relationships, but none compared to Rose Verbeck.

Rose, even when we first met as children, has always had a unique sense of humor, an unconventional personality, and a sarcastic wit about her. She may come off as indifferent, but she's actually really good-natured and kind. A natural beauty that effortlessly draws you to her.

Might draw you in and then push you off a cliff, but hey, that's a risk I'll take.

The shift is dragging as I keep one eye on the door. I don't want to miss her when she walks in. There's got to be a way to win her friendship back. I'm hoping once I explain what happened all those years ago, she'll see that I'm not her enemy. Tonight, I'm hoping this will be my second chance.

"You're on edge. What's bothering you?" Niko asks me as he pours some brandy into his coke.

"Do you remember Rose?" I knock my knuckles against the granite bar countertop.

"Verbeck's daughter? *Your* Rose? *The* Rose." I nod. Niko laughs and shoves the bottle into my chest. "Here. You need this."

"What's that supposed to mean?" I take the bottle and frown at him.

"You screwed up last time. Drink this. Don't think. Be honest. Don't screw it up again."

He takes his drink and walks away still chuckling to himself.

The place begins to get busy, but I still look over every second, every breath I take to see if she's there. Normally I'd be thrilled at how many of my drink specials are being ordered for Sweetest Day, but right now, all I can focus on is that I'm mixing this drink for everyone *but* her.

Our hostess, Petra, groans as her whole body droops against the bar. I'm drying a glass as I tell her, "That's not the Christmas spirit. You're typically holly and jolly. What's up?"

"She is *The Nightmare before Christmas* embodiment, and just walked in. This girl is the adult version of Wednesday Addams with only a borderline goth look."

The side of the granite bar digs into my stomach as I lean over to stretch my neck as far as I can to see Rose. *Who else would she be describing in Candy Cane Key?*

There, standing in the doorway, is my Rose. She's wearing an oversized plain black tee that hangs off her right delicate shoulder, and ripped jeans with black Converse. I typically don't pay much attention to what people are wearing, but she's such a contrast to everyone else.

I tap the counter in front of Petra. "I got it. Hold

down the fort here for a bit, yeah? Please." Her eyebrows disappear behind her bangs, but she gives me a nod. I hop on top of the bar and then slide off the other side. I rush over to greet her at the host station. "Hello." I say, a bit out of breath. "Welcome to Niko's Taverna. Will you be sitting on the naughty or nice side?"

She crosses her arms and stares me down. After a bit she arches a brow. I accept that's the only answer I'm getting so I say, "Naughty it is." I reach out and pluck one of her hands free, and with a smirk say, "Let me take you to the naughty and fun side of things."

Her lips part, and I see a spark in her eyes. She quickly recovers and schools her expression, but I saw it. *I caught that, Rose.* She got my double meaning, and a part of her was interested. There's hope for me after all. But I have to go slow, so I show I'm respecting her boundaries, and not being pushy. However, not too slow because she's leaving in a couple of days. Her agreeing to sit with me now is a huge step forward. Progress, we're making progress.

I lead her to the best booth in the house. I made sure nobody used it. It's more secluded, romantic, tucked away in a little corner with an oceanfront window, and near a column with twinkling lights that provide a soft glow. "How about this booth?" Her sliding into the booth I'm going to take as a yes. "I'll, um, go get our drinks."

Flirting and communicating with people is all part

of being a good bartender. And I'm a *damn* good one. So why am I running from Rose right now? Because I'm nervous as hell, and her strong poker face is intimidating. I hurry behind the bar where Petra is busy.

"Did you come to rescue me?"

I hate to shut down her hopeful expression. "No. I'm going on break."

"*Break?*" She looks up and spots Rose. "For *her?* Thanasis, forgive me, but why? Wanting to take a walk on the dark side? What's the deal? You could literally have your pick of any woman." She smirks at me and tosses ponytail. "Any woman…"

"Let's hope that's true, because I want that one."

"I'll never understand you."

"Shhh. I need to focus." I can feel her rolling her eyes behind me. I grab fresh figs that I brought from my own yard. I use top shelf products, no second tier for Rose. Not that I think she'll care, but I want to know I'm providing her with the best. I place the two cocktails on a serving tray, along with a plate of fresh figs, some pita chips, and cucumber sauce with fresh Kalamata olives and dill on top. "There. Wish me luck. Oh and send a server over in a bit to get our order."

"Do I need to send a priest, or exorcist, as well?"

"Really? Only because she's not bubbly and wearing bright colors?"

"If she turns out to be a vampire and kills you, can I be promoted to manager?"

"No."

"Why?"

"Because you judge our customers based on their appearance."

I smile at customers as I pass. A few call out to me and wave. My hands are trembling as I place the drink in front of Rose. "Care for a drink, neighbor?" I try to cover up my nervousness by being flirty and playful.

Another server appears to take my tray after I place everything on the table. She sniffs the drink and then looks at me.

"Go ahead. I might be your taste." I tease her.

"Doubtful." The gleam appears in her eyes again so I know that sharp tongue is about to cut me in two. Excitement fills me. "I don't care when things are… overdone."

Is she saying I'm overdone? Maybe I'm a little much. I like that she doesn't sit across from me and fill me with compliments, giggles, and plays coy. I wink at her as I pick up my glass. "Cheers."

My eyes zero in on her lips touching the rim of the glass. The purple liquid slides between her dark red lips. A sweet delicious moan slips out. I wonder if that's the same sound she'd make if it were me to slide between those red lips.

"I'll admit, it's not terrible. I could at least swallow it down." *She loves it.* My chest puffs out and I'm feeling pretty good about myself.

"I'm sure there's other areas you might find not so terrible, if you'd give them a chance."

"Are you talking about this tropical Christmas town or you?"

"Both."

"Both are ridiculous. I just haven't decided which one is more so."

She's flirting with me. This is happening. I'm going to get my second chance. "Both of us spread joy. What's so ridiculous about that?"

"Isn't Christmas supposed to be cold with snow? A white Christmas? *Let it Snow, Let it Snow, Let it Snow.*"

"Jesus was born in the Middle East. Palm trees. Warm climate."

I'm slightly offended at how surprised she looks. "That is actually a valid point. But I still feel like this place is using the holiday just as a year-round scheme."

"It's a town that likes to have fun and celebrate Christmas more than one month out of the year."

"So you're going to ignore all the other holidays for the sake of this one?"

I hold up my cocktail glass. "We've been celebrating Sweetest Day all day."

"I've never seen anyone celebrate Halloween. Or anything spooky."

"I wouldn't, even if I didn't leave here. Skeletons are creepy. Spiders. Ghosts. No thanks. If I wanted to look at a graveyard year round, I would've moved across from the cemetery."

Rose giggles. It's not a mocking one, but it's genuine. "They won't come to me if I don't use their full names."

Whoa. This is a change of direction so I lean forward. "I'm sorry? Who?"

"Tiny… " Rose looks up to the ceiling and then sighs. Her eyes find mine and she forces the names out. "Tiny Tim. And Ebenezer."

"Well, yeah. Most people expect you to use their name when addressing them."

"It's annoying. They're little monsters."

"You don't like them for having self-respect?"

"Also, my parents must be spending a fortune on their toys and fancy food."

It must be the bartender in me that has her opening up and venting, sharing her problems with me. Not the conversation I was hoping for - I didn't even see this one coming - but we're talking. I take a sip and then tell her. "They have standards. Top shelf quality."

"Their little black beady eyes are always watching me. Like two little demon pups."

"Of course they're watching you. What are they supposed to do? You're in their house. Wait – that's it." I can't stop the smile from spreading across my face. "You're jealous." Rose gives me a scowl, and looks at me like I'm a ridiculous immature child. Which proves I'm right. She only gets this defensive when I've struck a nerve. "You. Are. Jealous. Of two five pound chihuahuas."

Rose taps her nails against the cocktail glass. "Hardly. Anyways, this drink is lovely, but I probably need to get back."

"Wait. Try the figs." I slice the fig in half. Revealing the pink sweet center. I gently take my finger to caress around the edges, and then to the little hole in the center. The entire time I keep my eyes trained on Rose. Her nostrils flare. Lust fills her eyes. My third finger is covered in sweet juice. "I'd like to have a taste." I suck the nectar from my finger. I hold the fig half out to her, but she declines with a slight shake of her head. "Afraid you might enjoy it?"

Not allowing her to lose eye-contact with me, I run my tongue along the center of the fig. I lick and eat the center of the fig as though it's her center I'm devouring. Rose shifts in her seat, crossing her legs. A slight flush creeps up her neck and colors her cheeks. She's thinking about it as well. So easily this could be her.

"I have to go."

Before I can stop her, Rose is darting through the restaurant and out the door. Well… it's a start. I'm not giving up yet, Rose Verbeck.

Chapter Five

Rose

The nerve of him. Attempting to seduce me by violating that fruit. He hasn't changed at all. Also, when did the fig become so sexual? Can a fruit be sexy? It was. At first it looked like a ball sack but once sliced it reminded me of a vagina. *And then how he used his tongue on it...* The fig is officially a fuckable fruit.

No. Oh my gosh. No. Ew. It's simply been a long day and I am not going to think about Thanasis tongue punching the inside of a fig. He has really gotten under my skin. Pet play dates. Convincing me to drink his delicious *Gettin' Figgy* drink. Oral sex with a fig. I bet he's having a good laugh about all this. Little miss uptight grumpy Rose. I bet he's getting a thrill toying with me.

I slow the car down as I approach my parents' house. I look over at the blinding lights of Thanasis Christmas decorations *in* October. *What a monstrosity.* And just like that... I feel like the Grinch. Because it's about to become a real monstrosity. A wickedly wonderful monstrosity.

Today is going to be a beautiful day. My feet bounce as I sing *Banana Boat (Day-O)* to the kitchen to pour a cup of coffee. I even pet and sing to Tiny Tim and Ebenezer. After I add some creamer, I sit down with my cup and smile back at the set of brown eyes looking at me. "Hear me out. How about Beetle and Juice? Wouldn't those be fun names?"

Tiny Tim barks at me. I wrinkle my nose, "You could be Juice if you don't like Beetle."

He doesn't look convinced. I doubt they'd go for Jack and Skeleton either. Michael and Myers? Pumpkin and Spice?

"What about Trick and Treat?"

"What are you planning on them becoming, strippers, or porn stars?" I scream at the deep voice that came from the window. *Tha-ASS-hole.* Of course.

"What are you doing creeping by my parents' kitchen window?"

"One it was open. And two, I assumed you liked surprises. Being scared. Pranks and such."

A wicked smile plays on my lips. He's seen his front yard. "I thought the deflated snowmen with the gremlin's holding blow dryers was funny."

"Gremlins? That's what you'd turned my elves into? I thought they were demons."

"It was dark. My makeup might've been off. But come on, I went to the store to purchase extra blow dryers for that gag. They were melting the snowmen, get it?"

Thanasis doesn't look amused. "You know kids live on this street. Stringing the lights to look like Santa is peeing off the side of the house isn't appropriate. And having my other elves holding a body bag with the rest of my Christmas decorations in it is borderline disturbing."

I can't help it. I snort with laughter. Thanasis' eyes soften and I notice a slight twitch at the corner of his mouth. "I wanted us to become friends. To make peace."

Doubtful. But I'll play along. "Fine. Let's be friends."

"Too late. You don't mess with a man's yard." I scoff. Thanasis continues. "I want you to remember you started this."

Started what? Uh oh. "Nothing has started. It's finished. Consider that as me getting even for last night."

"What happened last night?"

"You were being obscene." I hate the way my eyes drift to his lips. His perfect teeth are on display with his sexy knowing smile. His tongue snakes out only a little bit to wet his lips, but it's enough to have me squeezing my thighs together.

"And you're being childish by vandalizing my property."

"Is it vandalizing if it's an improvement? When you think about it, I did you a favor. Consider it my gift to you for Sweetest Day."

"You definitely spiced up the neighborhood. I'll see you for our playdate." I hate that he looks so sexy when he winks. I wonder if I can teach the dogs to pee on him.

I spend the afternoon decorating my parents' front yard for Halloween. Nobody else has decorated, well other than Thanasis' house of course. I get a rush every time I look over at his front yard. I don't do a lot because I won't be here to take it down, but I can't resist putting up a little bit. It baffles me that they want to live where it's always warm, and the town's theme is the winteriest of winter holidays. This will be a nice little surprise for them too since they didn't warn me about their neighbor.

I hear a door open and shut and look over to see Thanasis walking over with Figs. He's wearing a very nice pair of jeans and a plain white crew neck shirt. Of course he makes average clothes look like he's on a fashion runway.

"There's my favorite Scrooge." He says with a huge grin.

"How about you go scrooge yourself?"

"Hey we have little ears present. Don't use that kind of language around my son." He actually looks down at Figs and loudly whispers, "You don't repeat that. We don't use such language do we? No we don't. Good boy."

Despite the exchange being completely endearing, I fake disgust. "Well now we know why you're single."

"Oh, were you wondering about that? I knew you'd been thinking about me."

"I think I should suggest to my parents to extend the fence to their front yard as well."

"I agree. Keep you out of my yard. You little vandal."

I can't stop myself from laughing. Instead of continuing this foolish conversation I go to the house to retrieve Tiny Tim and Ebenezer. We go through the process of choosing their collars and outfit to wear out. I put their leashes on since we're walking out the front door. "Let's go, gentlemen."

"Tiny Tim and Ebenezer! Figs, look! It's your best friends." Thanasis crouches down to pet the canine trio as they're sniffing each other. He looks up at me and asks, "Wanna take them for a walk along the beach?"

"As in you and I take a stroll along the beach?"

"It would include us. Yes. Because… we're… walking these guys. I'm simply suggesting we walk them on the beach." He stands and holds a hand up. "Don't complicate it. It's not like we're going to be holding hands."

"I didn't say I wanted to hold your hand!"

"You did, with your eyes, and that defensive tone." He gently tugs Figs' leash and tells him to come along. I do the same with my two. We walk in silence. The three leading the way get extremely excited, practically dragging us, as soon as the beach comes into view.

"We had some good times here." Thanasis says. "Did you bring a swimsuit? I remember you used to always wear a black one with white polka dots."

I narrow my eyes at him and purse my lips together. As I recall, he told his friends that I glowed in the water because I was so pale. They called me "*glow worm.*" So I began to call him Tha-nasty. Yet my nickname didn't stick with the crowd of friends like his nickname for me did. Some of the girls that were meaner, and jealous of any attention he gave me, shortened my nickname to 'worm.' The guys would call out, "Hey there's Thanasis' Glowworm." Some got it wrong and would say, "Glow Stick." Either way it was humiliating and insulting.

I reached my breaking point when my parents pushed me into entering the Christmas karaoke contest at Niko's Taverna. I couldn't even finish the song because they kept shouting those stupid nicknames. There I was with a freaking spotlight on me as everyone in there laughed, and called me a degrading name. Taunting me for my pale skin and narrow frame. After that, I never wanted to be in this obnoxious little town again. The worst part is, I used to love coming here. I had loved Thanasis, too.

But that was twelve years ago. I don't ever want to discuss that mortifying chapter of my life. That's where I fear this conversation is going now and I refuse to allow it. I ignore his comment about my bikini, and only answer him about if I have a swimsuit. "No."

"Who comes to the Keys and doesn't plan to swim?"

"I said I don't have a swimsuit. I didn't say I wasn't planning on swimming."

Thanasis' mouth pops open. I decide to leave him that way. I gently tug on Tiny Tim's and Ebenezer's leash and say, "I think we've had enough. Goodbye."

Chapter Six

Thanasis

Rose doesn't show up to Niko's. I keep thinking she might, but a part of me isn't completely surprised either. I don't let it get me down. I still do my job. Serve incredible drinks. Help the servers seat customers and carry out plates. Flirt when necessary. Crack jokes. Then go in the back and help wash dishes.

I know she still hates me from when I was an insecure and stupid teenager. I've loved Rose since we were kids. Even as a kid, I knew she was different. I loved how different she was, because I was different too, being raised by Greek immigrants. As we entered our teens, she really did blossom. My guy friends started to notice. Jealousy began to get to me. She lived far away, and was only mine temporarily, for the times they came for vacation. Worse, I never knew where I stood with her. Friend? Boyfriend? The name Rose matches her personality. She has a timeless beauty and appears delicate, but she has a strong stem and thorns. She can withstand a storm, and will draw blood.

Growing up in a family that was always busting each other's balls, I honestly didn't think she'd get so upset when I teased her about how her skin looked like it was glowing in the water. It was only meant for her to hear. I called her a little glowworm. Tiny. Beautiful. Unique and rare. Hell, she looked more like a siren. But I wasn't going to be that forward with her. I always had to cover myself around her because I was afraid I'd poke her eye out. Or humiliate myself if she saw my boner and didn't think I was big enough. God, I had so many insecurities. I teased her, thinking I was being playful, but others heard me. They were quick to join in. It got out of hand, and I didn't stop it. I didn't tell them to shut up, or to fuck off. She ignored me for a couple of days. I was working at the club when she came in with her parents. When she went on that stage my heart was beating so fast with excitement. However, it turned out to be the night I lost her. The group of jerks from the beach started catcalling and yelling "glowworm," "glowstick," and "worm." Turns out they'd been giving her a hard time every time they saw her. She didn't even get to finish

Gettin' Figgy

her song, and I didn't get to say goodbye. Twelve-years later she's back in my life.

I need this second chance. She's not going to come back into Niko's. However, her parents leaving her to tend to their fur babies works in my favor. We have our playdates, and I intend to make the most of it.

But first, I need to fix my yard... and hers.

There's a chance I'm going overboard, but I can be a little competitive. I repainted an old sign we'd had with an arrow pointing toward the restaurant. Instead of Niko's, it now says Grinch's Lair, and is pointing toward Rose's house. Her skeletons all have Santa and Elf hats now. I painted the pumpkins white and stacked them to be friendly snowmen, complete with glitter thrown on them. Her ghosts have been wadded up and turned into hanging snowballs, or sheets of snow on the trees, porch, and mailbox. Lucky for her I have tons of extra white lights. Her house can be seen from miles away. I'm surprised the blinding lights didn't wake her.

I'm beyond exhausted by the time I walk through my front door. I crash on the couch because I lack the energy to make it to my bedroom. Figs jumps on me and licks my face. "Let's get some sleep, Buddy. Because tomorrow, we're going to have a very angry neighbor. Yeah. There might be some tension during playdate. But know that this has nothing to do with you, Tiny, and Eb. We love you very much."

I'm beyond delirious from exhaustion. But. It. Was. Worth. It.

Bang! Bang! Bang! "Open this door! Than-*ASS*-es! Open up!" *Bang! Bang! Bang!*

Despite the rude wake up call, I get off the couch wearing a giant grin. I open the door and lean against the frame. "*Gooood* morning sunshine."

"If you don't wipe that smug look off your face, I cannot guarantee your safety."

"Are you threatening me?"

"I'm hanging on by a thread. Consider it a word of caution."

"Stop. You're going to upset Figs."

Rose points toward her yard. "What have you done? I thought we had a truce."

"I believe we'd reached somewhat of an understanding, but no truce."

"Fine." Rose turns around and stomps off my porch. On the way to her house, she calls over her shoulder, "War it is."

I can't stop smiling as I wave to her. She's so adorable when she's angry. I should probably be terrified, yet I'm completely bewitched by the she- devil. "See you on the battlefield."

I close the door to begin my morning routine.

Stretch. Go for a jog with Figs. Breakfast. Shower and groom. Get dressed. Respond to work messages. Filter through hookup messages. However, now that Rose is back, I'm not interested in any of them.

She's not staying. I'm not foolish enough to think I'll win her over in the next couple of days. If I could at least get us to be on speaking terms, there might be hope for something in the future.

Hope.

That's what I love about living in a Christmas town. The whole town believes in joy, peace, and hope. I need that encouragement of faith more than anything right now. There has to be hope that Rose will give me a second chance.

Chapter Seven

Rose

I'd be okay with never seeing his stupid handsome face ever again. But since I'm stuck here a few more days, I'm going to be a thorn in his side. *Oh God. Did I just make a pun?* I've been here too long.

I need to get out as soon as my parents return. Before I leave, I need to leave my mark. What could I do to really annoy Thanasis?

He easily knows how to annoy me… Or so he thinks. This all started on Sweetest Day. What if I made *every* day Sweetest Day. He won't know how to act. I'll be sugary sweet during the day, but at night I'll still rearrange his yard. It'll be like flipping a switch.

After I transformed my yard from holly jolly vomit to pleasantly spooky, I went to get ready for the playdate. I didn't stop grooming, pampering, or dollin' myself up until I looked like an irresistible playmate. My hair had extra shine and volume. I took great care in applying my makeup to have the right amount of natural and seductive girl next door vibe. Today's outfit is casual but fitted. Enough effort was put in to make me look pretty, but not enough to be over the top obvious.

Before I can walk out the door with Tiny Tim and Ebenezer, my phone rings. "Hey Mom!" *Traitor.* "How are you and dad getting along?"

My mother's voice is cautious, and too high, as she speaks, "Good, good. Just fine dear. Tell me... how did Sweetest Day go?"

A snarky comment is on the tip of my tongue. I purse my lips together tightly and count to ten. This was her plan all along. I bet Thanasis has fooled my parents, with his charm, into thinking he's this wonderful guy. Knowing my mother she wants nothing more than to believe him because he's single and lives next door to her. If she thinks he's the key to get me to move here, and next door to her, she's about to be severely disappointed.

"It was... sweet." I say the last word too high pitched.

There's an awkward silence, and then my mother clears her throat. "Did you meet Figs?"

"Of course. Tiny Tim and Ebenezer had a playdate."

"Did you meet Figs' owner?"

"Mom," I say brightly, "just come out and ask. You want to know if Thanasis and I had a playdate as well."

At least her voice sounds somewhat guilty when she asks, "Well?" She should feel guilty. I deserved to have a heads up on seeing Thanasis again after twelve years.

"We did. We've talked. Even went out for a drink. In fact he's waiting for me, TT, and Eb."

"Who?"

"The dogs have long names. TT and Eb are their nicknames."

"You're not mad at me, are you?"

My voice turns high, and it's painful to keep myself from exploding. "Why would I be mad?"

"I know you used to have a crush on Thanasis, and he called you names. But he's a man now. A mature and very nice young man. He's single, too."

And there it is.

"Being single doesn't mean I'm desperate. You raised me to be a woman with morals and standards. I don't settle. No matter how single I am."

"I'm proud of you. Yes, I did. I'll trust your judgment on this sweetheart. But do me a favor, I also raised you to have an open mind, keep it open."

We say our goodbyes and love you's. I think about what she said. I do have an open mind. Right now it's open to all the possibilities of getting on Thanasis' last nerve.

Thanasis and Figs are standing by the back gate when TT, Eb, and I walk outside. He has to do a double take when he sees us. *Excellent.* I smile widely. "Hi Figs! Thanasis!" They both stare at me with wide eyes, and their ears perked up, as I sashay past them with TT and Eb.

Thanasis and his side-kick quickly catch up with us. "Should I be nervous?"

"Well that's a fine way to greet me." My facial muscles ache but the smile remains in place.

"You're right."

"I am?"

"Yes. That was rude. I'm sorry."

A frown threatens to tug at my lips. *Why is he being so agreeable? Freakin' Than-ASS-hole.* Well I should've known one friendly encounter wouldn't crack Mr. Ray of Sunshine.

Through the entire walk, I maintain a friendly and painfully sweet upbeat attitude. I'm terrifying myself. He, on the other hand, feeds off of it. The happier I appear, he ups it a notch. This whole walk is supposed to be me getting under his skin, a thorn in his side, but it's backfiring.

"I think these little cuties are starting to get thirsty. I better get them back." I've had enough of this. The walk back is, thankfully, silent until we reach the gate to our yard.

"How about we go out tonight?"

My brain malfunctions. I can't process the words I

just heard come out of his mouth. I hate how his hopeful brown eyes spark something inside of me. I'm still foolishly attracted to him. A slow evil smile spreads across my face. If my hair could curl it would be doing so, just like the Grinch's in the cartoon.

"How about," I take a step toward him and continue speaking, "we stay in?"

"In?"

"Yeah. I could swing by the Gumdrop Grocer. I'll cook for us."

"You're going to poison me."

"What? No!"

"Alright. I'm not touching any apples."

"I'm going to take that as a compliment. You see me as a queen."

"Sure. But I'll have Mohagen's Pizza on standby. Just in case."

I give him a wink. "Fair enough." I purposely touch him as I walk past through the gate. I feel ridiculous flirting this way, but oddly enough, it's working. Thanasis is looking at me like I'm on tonight's menu. And fudge, if I don't like it.

One thing I remember about Thanasis is he hates jalapeño. I doubt that has changed. The first thing I grab off the shelf in Gumdrop Grocer - a nice big can of jalapeños. Tonight's dish is going to be a creamy jalapeño cheese sauce over chicken and pasta. Excitement fills me as I grab all the ingredients that I need.

On my way home, I stop at The Ginger Bread Man. Cal, the owner, tends to sell out early, so it was a miracle I was able to snag a few cookies. A tiny shred of me is feeling guilty, so to balance it out and clear my conscience, I grab some of Thanasis favorite gingerbread cookies.

Tonight's dinner will be revenge… served on a warm plate, and made with pettiness.

Chapter Eight

Thanasis

She's up to something. Her girl next door routine was cute, and did give me a chubby, but I'm not so sure I should eat anything Rose gives me. She hates me. But that's going to change tonight. I'm going to explain everything if it's the last thing I do. Which it very well could be. My final words will be, "I'm sorry for calling you a glow worm."

I grab a few figs off the tree as I cross the yard to Rose's. I grabbed a bottle of vodka to whip us up some *Gettin' Figgy* drinks. Figs follows me as I walk across. "Maybe she'll finally see that I'm figgin' awesome." I tell him. He doesn't look convinced. "Or she'll tell me to fig off for good." He has the nerve to let his tongue out and smile up at me. I sigh. "Either way, tonight we'll *fig*ure it out." Figs barks and I agree.

I need to get a hold of myself. "I'm sorry. I'm nervous, and being cheesier than normal. I've got to get it together. Fudge. What am I going to do, Figs?" He gives me a little whimper. "Yeah. I know. It's not looking good. I'm already sweating like crazy. What if stink? Here boy, smell me." I crouch before Figs so he can sniff my neck and armpits.

"Whatcha doin' there?" *Why does the universe hate me?*

I look over to see Rose standing on her porch while Tiny Tim and Ebenezer are running around the yard. She's wearing a simple black dress with yellow Converse sneakers. Her hair hangs down in waves. Even from here I can see her makeup is minimal with the main focus being her red lips and black eyeliner. *Stunning.* Yet, here I am talking in puns to my dog, and letting him sniff me for sweat.

Standing up, I awkwardly chuckle at myself. "You weren't there a minute ago."

"They needed out." She gestures to the little dogs.

I mumble to myself. "Figures."

"What?"

"Nothing. I grabbed some figs for drinks. I have some of the best figs in Candy Cane Key. One might say they're a fig deal." *Elf my life.* Figs runs off, and I don't blame him.

"Sounds great. Come on in."

I step into the house and immediately am greeted with an incredible aroma. "It smells delicious."

Rose has a gleam in her eyes. "I hope you're hungry."

Fuuuuudge. It's poisoned. I knew it. "I am. But I want you to think long and hard about the consequences. I know you love October, Autumn, and Halloween… but do you want to wear orange for the rest of your life."

"I don't think I'd hate it." Her face is completely serious. Tonight might very well be my last meal unless I walk out that door. Then Rose does something completely unexpected.

She laughs. A genuine laugh. The combination of sound and beauty stops my heart. She may not have to poison me at all. This moment here is enough to do me in. Rose Verbeck has the loveliest laugh. The way her eyes and face light up when she gives an authentic smile. She's glowing. But I don't dare comment on it. I enjoy this rare and enchanting moment.

"Go sit down. If I was going to off you, it wouldn't be with poison."

"Good to know. It's not that you'd never murder someone, just not that method. Poison wouldn't be your choice of weapon."

I take a seat at the round dining table. Rose walks behind me and whispers in my ear, "You should feel special. I would never murder *anyone*, only you."

In a mock flattery I say, "Aw. So, I'm your someone." I turn my head and our faces are a breath apart. I can smell her perfume. She has tiny flecks of gray in her blue eyes. There're a few tiny freckles on her nose. Her lips look so sensual with that red coloring.

I'm going to kiss her. The more I stare at her mouth, the harder it's getting to resist. Over the years, I've thought about it so many times. All I need to do is lean forward the tiniest bit...

"Chicken's ready!" She shouts in my face before spinning around and sprinting into the kitchen. Plan has now progressed from getting a second-chance at friendship, to getting a second-chance for a kiss.

As soon as I take the first bite, I know what she's up to. And I'm truly touched. *She remembers.* Only someone who truly cared about you would remember the foods you hated. Rose prepared a dish with jalapeños. It's not like that's a common ingredient, so this isn't a mere coincidence. I'm so happy that I don't even care if my lips are burning - and it's not for wanting to kiss her, even though I desperately do. Honestly, this dish isn't even that bad. I'm actually enjoying it.

Rose thinks she's prepared a dish that I'm going to hate. She couldn't be more wrong. I love it. Not only is it delicious, despite the sauce having jalapeños, but this meal has proven there's hope for me yet.

I look over and see she's scowling at me. I cut a

slice of chicken, and then lather it in the sauce, before shoving it in my mouth. After a few chews I say, "This is scrumptious. What's in the sauce? I have to have the recipe."

Her lips part, and the surprised look on her face is comical. "It's cheese, cream, and jalapeños. Lots of spicy jalapeños."

"That's it. That spice gives it a kick. Clears your sinuses, too."

She taps her fork against her place. "Yup." She pops the 'p.' "So you…like it?"

"This cooking has me wanting to get jalapeño pants." I tease. She stares at me like I'm the biggest idiot she's ever met. Which is fair. What am I doing? I clear my throat. "Sorry. Bad joke."

"Let's keep it to only the food being spicy."

"Ouch." We eat for a bit in silence. My plate is almost clean, so I should probably bring up what happened twelve years ago to finally clear the air. "Twelve years ago, we had a misunderstanding."

Her fork rattles against the plate. "What are you doing?"

"I'm bringing up - "

"Something that happened twelve years ago. Now? You think now is a good time."

"There's never going to be a great time to discuss this. It's eating me up. Let me apologize."

"Oh." She crosses her arms. "It's bothering *you* so you only want to apologize so you can feel better. I should've added more jalapeños."

My chest puffs out. "I knew it. You remembered I hate them. That proves you care."

"I was secretly hoping your face would turn red and I'd see steam coming out of your ears. That was all I cared about."

I'm calling figgy pudding on that one. I'll let her have it though. It's time to move on. "I didn't mean for everyone to call you *glow worm*. I honestly didn't mean for it to be an insult. I saw glow worms one time in a cave. They were majestic. And they're rare. You, that day in the water, with the sun shining on you," I have to take a moment because the image is so vivid in my mind. "You were just as breathtaking, Rose. I said it before I thought. It was meant to be a term of endearment. But then the others heard. I didn't stand up to them. I didn't stop them. Which makes me a total tool." I inhale and exhale. Here comes the hard part. "Also… I might've been really insecure back then. I didn't want any of the other guys looking at you, or talking to you. A few I pushed away from you. But I swear, I never meant for them to harass you, or embarrass you. I didn't have anything to do with the girls."

"Yes, you did. They were falling at your feet, but since you had your sights set on ruining my life, they hated me."

"If I could go back, I would. I was a dumbass."

"Was?"

"I still keep messing up things between us. I promise if you'll give me a second chance at our friendship, I'll keep messing up, but I'll eat a jalapeño straight if it means you'll keep giving me more chances. Eventually, I'll either learn, or lose all taste buds."

We sit there a beat staring at one another. Without a word, she stands and disappears into the kitchen. She walks back out carrying a platter. "Oh. Oh, come on." I stare down at the best gingerbread men in the entire world. I immediately recognize these as Cal's signature gingerbread. I look back at Rose. "You really are up to snow good."

"Don't be rude-olph. Eat your figgin' cookies."

She made a pun. What's happening? Is she flirting with me? I can't resist the cookies so I quickly take one and stare at her as I bite the head off. It's so soft and chewy and absolutely perfect. "Why? You're freakin' me out. Why did you get these?"

"Maybe I was feeling… santa-mental."

I need to move. I need to do something. I'm seriously about to pounce on her. I can't deal with flirty, punny Rose. This is starting to remind me of who she was before I had to make everything weird and notice her boobs.

"How about I make us some *Gettin' Figgy* drinks?"

Rose places her hand on my shoulder and pushes me back down in my seat. "How about we get figgy?"

Say what? "Just to be clear. You don't mean we get my dog, or eat the actual fruit. You're doing a play on the word jiggy? Do you want to dance? Or is this an innuendo of sex?"

She tilts her head and furrows her brows. "What's going on with you?"

"I'm nervous! Okay? I'm so worried I'm going to mess this up. I'm confused. I'm horny. You're the only person I get this awkward around because you're the only one whose opinion I actually respect. Other than my family's, of course, but I'm not trying to fig them." Holly leaves and Christmas trees somebody help me. I am rambling and talking about incest. This is a disaster. I can literally flirt with anyone, but the one person I want. "I'm going to go."

I stand up. I'm there, right in front of Rose. Twelve years is a long time to pine after someone. Here she is. I've waited and hoped for this moment. It'd be so easy to cup her face and press our lips together. I've done it to countless other women. But she's the only one who would really count. Which is why I have to walk away. This isn't the right time. I can see in her eyes that she was really hurt. I did that. Doesn't matter if I intended for everyone else to bully her, they did it because of me. I called her that name that sent all of this spiraling out of control. I didn't put a stop to it. I didn't speak up. They were my circle of friends. I'm not sure how I'll ever win her forgiveness. I'll never forgive myself for being such a dumbass coward. But, one day, I'll have my second chance.

For now, I have to touch her. I gently trail the back of my fingers down her cheek. "Thank you. This was the best meal of my life."

"I doubt that." Her voice is barely above a whisper. "There were jalapeños."

"But you made it. And I shared it with you. Best meal of my life."

Her face is getting warm beneath my touch. I better go now before I do something stupid. I turn around and grab two gingerbread men. "Bye."

I bump into the chair and then trip on my own feet, but quickly regain my balance. I don't look back. I just hurry out of the house, calling for Figs. Not my finest moment, but I don't regret a single second because it was definitely the greatest moment in the last twelve years.

Chapter Nine

Rose

I don't even know what just happened. I was practically throwing myself at him, and he ran. What did I miss? This is what I get for allowing my emotions to get the best of me. He was being incredibly sweet, and I was eating it up. Then he ran. Was he only after the chase? The challenge, perhaps?

Well, I refuse to let the night be a total loss. My plan to sabotage his meal backfired. Time to go back to what works. I grab some supplies to take to his front yard.

I move all the snowmen together and give them little signs that read, "Strike!" "We want off during the Fall!" "October Vacations!"

Next, I string pink lights in the shape of a shaft

on the tree bark and wrap lights on the branches to resemble the tip of a penis. Then I take white lights and have them set to blink in stages so it looks like they are spewing out and down. The neighbors will love this. Maybe the police will come. *Ah, I made another pun!* I found some gnomes from the other neighbor's yard. I place them in his, and give them all makeovers to look like classic horror villains. I do the typical caution tape and spiderwebs.

I step back and look at my masterpiece. He's going to be so pissed. Tomorrow can't get here soon enough.

Thanasis doesn't knock on my door in the morning. He also doesn't show up for our playdate, leaving me to deal with a very upset Tiny Tim and Ebenezer. Who really is a scrooge when he's mad. They've been sulking all day.

A part of me should feel relieved I finally got to him. Mr. Ray of Sunshine isn't so happy now. I feel hollow and cold. My eyes keep drifting toward the window, but there's no sign of him, or Figs. Worse, the Halloween decorations are still up. Tomorrow my parents should arrive so this should be my victory. I managed to annoy Thanasis before their return and my departure.

I sit on the couch cuddled with Tiny Tim and Ebenezer all day, watching horror movies. They are quite the Stephen King fans. "How about I start calling you Stephen and King? Yeah? You like that? I do too." The doorbell rings, sending them into a frenzy. "It's okay my dear Stephen and King."

There's a young girl standing on the porch when I open the door. "Hello! I'm from Cocoa Corner, and I have a delivery for a Rose Verbeck."

"That'd be me."

"Sign here. And here you are. Enjoy!"

I accept the box of chocolates. There's no note. I call my mom immediately to ask if they're from her.

I can hear the smile in her voice. "No, sweetie. But who is sending you chocolates?"

The only other person this could be is…

This whole time I was worried I'd gone too far. That I'd let my grudge of twelve years get in the way of Thanasis trying to apologize. He explained himself. I was ready to forgive him then, but then felt rejected all over again when he left.

Should I go running up there just because he sent me a box of chocolates? I sit back on the couch as my only friends lick and cuddle me. I've never experienced a connection with anyone like I do with him. He explained it was all a misunderstanding. He had tried to apologize before, but I allowed my insecurities to prevent me from opening up to him again. This could be our second chance. The question is, am I ready to open myself up. Risk the heartache that comes with being vulnerable with another person.

I jump up from the couch, sending his majesty, King, barking again. He really isn't a fan of sudden movements - yet here he watches movies where they do that all the time. "I'm going to Niko's. Wish me luck boys!"

Heart palpitations. Sweaty palms and pits. Butterflies in my stomach. This was all a mistake. My body is screaming for me to abort this mission. I've at least made it through the door, so that's a positive. I can do this.

"Naughty or Nice?" The hostess asks me.

"The bar. Please."

"Extra naughty. You must be one of Thanasis' girls."

"I'm not one of... I'm *the one*." I stare her down, and the smirk from her face quickly vanishes. I'm not going to take the bait. I can recognize jealousy. She reminds me of the girls when I was a teenager.

Thanasis is charming the pants off two ladies sitting at the bar. Yet, now that I watch him, it's all fake. His eyes don't sparkle like they do when he speaks to me. The smile isn't as sincere. He's still entertaining to watch, and gorgeous, very charismatic.

He must feel my eyes because he turns in my direction. *There's that sparkle.* Thanasis holds a finger up to the ladies, and hurries over to me. "Rose. I'm surprised to see you. Glad. But surprised."

His uncle Niko comes hurrying over to us. "Rose, lovely to see you. Thanasis, I need to speak with you. It's urgent. Very important. Can't wait."

"Theo. No. Give me a minute."

"No, really. It'll only take two minutes." He holds up two fingers and gives me an uneasy smile.

Thanasis looks thoroughly irritated. "Whatever it is you can handle it, or it can wait. I'm going on break." He leans on the bar and looks into my eyes. "You have no idea how happy I am that you're here."

"Well, I was very surprised to receive your chocolates."

My heart sinks when I see the confusion all over his face. There's also a mix of hurt.

Niko elbows his nephew. "Yes! The ones you told me to order. Silly boy. You said, 'Theo, can you order chocolates for the girl I've been dreaming about since I was a teenager, but been too stupid to do anything?' And I say, 'I'm already on the phone with Cocoa Cafe.' You should now make her your fig drink, and dance."

"You ordered her chocolates?" Thanasis asks.

Niko holds his hands out. Clearly pleading with his nephew to play along. "You no listen. You asked me."

"No, I didn't."

The elderly man frowns. He begins to scold his honest nephew, and then begs him to see reason. "Well, you should've. But look, she's here, and you waste all your time arguing with me. Argue with her.

Then make up. Drink fig juice. Dance. And if you're really lucky, you won't have to just dream about her anymore." Niko leaves us and Thanasis looks sheepish.

"Greek families. They can't help interfering."

"Not just Greek. Look at my parents."

"Yeah about that. I didn't want to stir anything, but you know it was your mom's idea we let our dogs' celebrate Sweetest Day. I think she wanted to make sure that play date happened."

I suspected as much. But now, I'm not even mad about it. "Speaking of, can I get another *Gettin' Figgy?*"

It's time to face my fears. After a few - four - *Gettin' Figgy* cocktails, I feel confident enough to hit the stage. Tonight, I'm performing. This is going to be the greatest karaoke performance this town has ever seen. I don't think they're ready to witness such greatness.

I shall be singing "*What's This,*" from *A Nightmare Before Christmas*. It's going to be epic.

The stage is higher than I remember. The lights are hotter. Last time I hadn't downed four cocktails either. The music begins, and before I can make a sound, someone yells, "I recognize that glow. It's the worm!"

I'm missing my intro. My mouth is open, but no

words - no sound is coming out. It's so hot up here. I bet they can see the sweat beads gathering around my hairline and above my lip. I close my eyes and listen to the upbeat song. Jack Skeleton was in a place where he didn't exactly belong, but he found joy.

I swallow, and this time when I open my mouth, the music pours out of me. I allow myself to open up and have fun. The people mocking me can go fig themselves. Other people begin cheering me on. I feel free as I sing and move along the stage. It's not until the end of the song I realize they're gone.

Thanasis' other uncle, Giannis, stops me before I can leave the stage. Music begins and we fall into harmony singing Elvis Presley's rendition of *"Santa Bring My Baby Back To Me."*

This time, it's Thanasis that won't let me exit the stage. "Sing one with me, please?"

I'm having so much fun. I eagerly nod, and the diners cheer. I'm surprised Thanasis chose John Lennon's *"Happy XMas (War is Over)."*

He leans in and whispers, "Don't tell Giannis, but I'm more of a Beatles fan."

As we sing, everyone fades away. It's so cliche, but true. I only look at him as I feel the music. His voice is so smooth and rich. It caresses me. This moment is so intimate and raw.

When the song ends, everyone is on their feet cheering, on both the naughty and nice sides.

Thanasis takes my hand, and drags me off the stage and through the double doors. Before I'm even aware of where I am, my back is against the building and his lips are on mine. This is borderline obscene. His body is pressed fully against mine and I can feel every part of him. He wants me as much as I want him, or at least his body does. But I want to feel more. I need more.

Thanasis pulls his lips from mine. His hands tighten their hold on my hips as he rocks into me. Every. Hot. Inch. That's bulging from his pants. There's a low rumble from his chest that has me needing more friction. He studies my face that he's cupped in his hand. "There's nothing I want more than for us to take this further. I've thought about kissing you every day."

"Stop thinking and start doing." I beg him.

"Rose." I'm not too thrilled about his tone. "Tonight's not the night."

"Why? And why is it only your decision?"

"Because I want a real second chance. If we jump into this after a few drinks, you might regret it tomorrow. I don't want to be your regret. I want to be your chance for forever."

Tears begin to swell in my eyes. My lower lip trembles as mixed emotions are tearing me apart. He wraps his hand around the back of my hand and brings me to his chest. My nipples are hard, my clit is throbbing with need, and my heart is melting, but my pride feels the sting of rejection. I hate and love him for this.

"Let me take you home. I'm sure the little guys need out."

I sniffle. "They don't like being alone at night."

He leans his forehead against mine. "I don't either."

"Wanna bring Figs over, and we all keep each other company?" My legs are shaky and the ache between my legs is desperate for his touch. This is probably a bad idea. I'm almost certain of it.

His tone is smug as he says, "Absolutely."

Chapter Ten

Thanasis

Warmth is wrapped all around me. Rose is in her adorable fuzzy pumpkin and black cat pajamas. One leg, and an arm, is thrown over me. Three furry little bodies are scattered on either side of us, with one at my feet. I'm trapped, but I couldn't be happier.

Rose releases a soft little sigh and rubs herself closer to me. Her face is so soft and delicate in the morning light. With great care not to disturb any of the other bed guests, I reach over with my right arm and run my fingers through her silky hair.

Her eyelashes flutter. "What time is it?" She asks with a sleep filled voice.

"I don't know. Morning."

She stretches her arm and tries to turn only to

receive a growl. "Oops." Then she tries to move the leg that's over me, and gets another complaint in the form of a growl. "We're trapped." She whispers to me.

"I'm okay with it." I confess.

"You won't be. I have to pee."

"You can't hold it a little longer? We're all comfortable."

"Nope." She pops the p. "Sorry guys."

With mock frustration, I call for them to go to the door.

After taking the three bosses out to do their business. I walk back into the room to find Rose standing in the hallway. "Hello, welcome to Verbeck's. Would you like to be on the nice list?" She gestures toward the living room. Her tongue darks out and wets her lips and then she sucks them in before asking, "Or the naughty list." With her other hand she gestures back to her bedroom.

She's not hungover. Rose is offering herself to me completely sober. If she leaves, I'm not sure I'll survive after having her. Not sure if that's better than spending the rest of my life always wondering what might've happened. I know I'll regret not following through with this.

I take the outstretched hand that's gesturing toward her room. And then I lead her to the bed. Twelve years I've fantasized about this moment. I've prayed for it. It's been at the top of my wishlist, Christmas list, bucket list - all the lists! Here we are.

All my insecurities are racing through my mind, but I shove them down. I've waited too long not to be present in the moment with her.

My movements are slow, giving her plenty of time to stop me at any point, as I remove her clothing. I toss my clothes to the side as well. I stare down at the length of her torso in front of mine as I trace her curves. "You're sure?"

"I've never hated you. I wanted to. I told myself I did."

"Wow. You're really boosting my ego. As glad as I am to hear that the woman who I'm hoping to have sex with doesn't hate me, are you sure about that?"

"Never. I couldn't."

I step closer, my cock touching the warmth of her body. "Are you saying I'm so irresistible that you can't hate me?"

"Maybe."

I want to ask if this is my second chance, the start of forever, or only for today. Instead I allow our bodies to take over. I become consumed with the feel of her against me. We don't break our kiss as we climb onto the bed together. She hums against me as my cock slides against her clit over and over. We're both already hot and wet. I angle her hips to find her entrance. This is it.

I force myself not to rush. My arms are shaky as I hold my weight above her and try to maintain control. The connection that I feel for her already has me about to explode - which would be extremely embarrassing. I have to make this last. She groans and tightens her body around me as I slide all the way in. The sensation is already too much. This is the best sex of my life and it's only been two pumps. It's been a while, but it hasn't been that long since I've been with a woman. It's all Rose. It's the power she has over me.

"I need you, Thanasis. Please don't stop. Please." Her lips tenderly caress my neck. She leans back and our eyes connect. The experience of being inside her and staring into her eyes… I've never felt anything like this. This is a moment I'll remember for the rest of my life.

With a deep and purposeful thrust, I try to pour everything I'm feeling into her. We both moan in pleasure as I continue to push and pull, over and over. Rose is being completely open and vulnerable with me. It's like I can feel all her emotions and read her so easily right now. It feels like a reflection of my own nervousness, fears, pleasure, and desire. Her body begins to contract around me.

Breathing is becoming extremely difficult. She squeezes me so tight, and her little cries of pleasure sound in my ear. The bed is hitting the wall. Our bodies are slick with sweat. Both of us are in a frenzy lost to passion. I lean down and begin to whisper against the side of her face. "Rose. Rose. You're so incredible. Rose."

"I know, baby. I know."

My need for her is overwhelming. I'm worried I'm being too forceful and rough with her because I'm officially a man consumed. Her body tightens around mine. She cries out and that sends me over. My release pours into her.

I collapse on the bed next to her and struggle to catch my breath. Then I turn my head to look at her, and she seems to be struggling to breathe as well. "What do you mean, you know? You know you're incredible, huh?"

We both laugh and turn on our sides to face one another. She playfully smacks my shoulder. "I mean - I know. I was feeling it too. It was incredible."

"It really was. And you really are."

Chapter Eleven

Rose

Barking comes from the living room, followed by the sound of a car door. I jump out of bed and scramble around to grab some clothes. "Leave. Leave! You have to leave."

Thanasis raises up on his elbows. "What? Why?"

"My parents are home! Shoo! Be gone!"

He has the nerve to laugh. "We're adults. Relax. I'll get dressed, but I don't have to sneak out of the house."

"They're going to ask questions as to why you're here."

"Because we're… well, what are we Rose?"

I'm not prepared to have this conversation. I'm

not completely sure what we are because I'm leaving tomorrow. Or tonight. Maybe tonight. "I'm asking you to please allow me to visit with my parents first, before explaining anything."

He jerks his arms through his shirt and scoffs. After he buttons his jeans, he walks out without a word, or a backward glance. I'm sure I somehow offended him, but this is new for me. I've never introduced my parents to any guy. It's an awkward situation to explain I was shagging their neighbor while housesitting. My mother will probably be thrilled.

I rush to the living room to greet my parents. Of course they have to give affection to my fur siblings. "What is this?" My father asks as he reads the tag hanging from the collar. "Stephen?"

Mother looks at the one she's holding. "King? Well you are royalty. Yes you are. May I kiss his majesty? May I? Oh my precious little ruler."

Father doesn't look quite as amused. "Not only did you redecorate the yard but you renamed our pets?"

"Oh Honey. They're bonded. See? I think it's wonderful. Tell me, did you bond with anyone else while we were gone?" My mother's smug smile has me blushing.

"Honey!" My father is more uncomfortable than anyone with this conversation.

A nauseous and sinking feeling has overcome me. I did bond with Thanasis. I have a real connection with him. This is scary. I've spent so long avoiding this town, and him, and now there's no reason to. He has been missing me as much as I have him. To know he looked forward to all our moments together as much as I did back then, and now, it changes everything.

I have a life back home. A lonely life. My parents are here. The man I love is here. Stephen, King, and Figs are here. It's starting to sound more like this is home than the empty house that holds my mailing address.

No.

"Well, I need to hit the road." I announce.

My parents are extremely disappointed that I have to leave immediately. But I'm about to do something rash, and I'm not a spontaneous person. I don't even stop to tell Thanasis goodbye. If that makes me a coward, so be it.

The radio station taunts me with Christmas songs that I continue to skip. Eventually I give up and turn it off. That's not helping. My mind keeps playing images and moments from before, and now. All full of happiness. My happiest moments have been shared in Candy Cane Key. I'm driving from a town I despise with tears in my eyes, because I don't want to leave. I shouldn't want to stay there. I shouldn't want *him*. But Kris Kringle, I do.

I want to spend every Sweetest Day in Candy Cane Key. Every Halloween, and yes, especially every Christmas. I want to spend them with Thanasis. A future of arguing over yard decorations and puns sounds amazing. It sounds like the happily ever after I've always wanted, but was too stubborn to admit.

I'm making a mistake.

I turn around and drive back in the direction of Candy Cane Key. I call Niko to request a favor. Before it's too late, I'm going to take some risks. I want a second chance. I want forever.

I sneak in the back door of Niko's, and thanks to Niko himself, I'm able to get to the karaoke stage undetected by Thanasis.

However, as soon as I'm on the stage, I feel his eyes on me. He must've heard that I'd left because I see the look of surprise and confusion on his face. Then I notice my parents sitting at the bar across from him. Yup. He heard the news.

I clear my throat and wait for the music to begin. Then I begin to sing *I'll Be Home For Christmas.*

My parents and Thanasis look at one another, and then at me. I nod and smile. My mom covers her mouth with her hands. My father looks on the verge of tears. And Thanasis… he has a smug smile that I'll have to take care of later. Might have to use my lips.

When the song is over, Thanasis is waiting for me next to the stage. "What was that about?"

"I'll be home for Christmas."

"Where's home, Rose?"

I wrap my arms around him and lay my head on his chest. "This is home."

Epilogue

ONE YEAR LATER

Rose

We've been back from our honeymoon for one week. It was spent in Salem, Massachusetts. Everything has come full circle. Our wedding was celebrated on Sweetest Day.

Last night I had set out skeletons all through the yard. Everywhere. In the trees, on the porch, at the mailbox, coming out of the ground, tending to the plants, climbing the fence, and anywhere I could position one. I'm so eager for my new husband to walk out and see what I did to our yard.

Thanasis walks into the kitchen for his morning coffee. I can't stop smiling and bouncing on my feet. "Good morning, husband."

"Good morning, wife." He gives me a slow sensual kiss. It almost makes me forget about my skeleton village in the yard. *Almost.*

"I think Figs wants to go for a walk." My tone just gave me away. It's too high. I'm hardly ever this excited.

"What did you do?" He starts running toward the front door.

Here we go!

I giggle - actually giggle - as I follow after him. When I step outside, I'm as surprised as he appears to be. "I like it!" He tells me. "The skeletons with Santa hats and lights. Mixing both holidays. Cute."

"Did you do this?" I point a finger at him.

"What? No."

I stare at all my hard work that's been taken over by the Christmas spirit. Two skeletons are even kissing while holding a mistletoe. The lights begin changing and then music starts playing. I look over to find my dad standing on his porch holding some kind of remote control and a cup of coffee.

"Hey there neighbors."

Thanasis purses his lips together and nods. "You know they were great neighbors before you moved in."

"They're in- laws now. That changes things." I tease. "You ready to fig up their yard?" I ask him, completely not teasing.

"Not how I was planning to spend our night, but okay."

"You come to the dark side and I'll do all kinds of tricks and treats."

"I do love being on the naughty list." He looks

over at my dad. "Good morning, Mr. Verbeck." And then mumbles to me. "That poor man. I'm going to destroy his yard just so I can jingle my bells with his daughter." Then he looks at our yard. "But we can keep this, right? I do really like it."

I can't help but laugh. "Yes. Unless the neighbors mess it up."

"Again, they were good neighbors - "

"Shush. Let's go plot our revenge on their yard over a glass of *Gettin' Figgy*."

Thanasis wraps his arm around me and kisses my forehead. "Fig cocktails do go best with diabolical plans."

We wave bye to my mischievous parents as we go back inside. I honestly couldn't be happier being home, especially for the holidays.

The End.

Also By Gail Haris

The Randall Series

Stolen Hearts

Forbidden Kisses

Unspoken Desires

K.O. Romance Series

Worth a Shot

My Best Shot

A Clear Shot

The Check In Series

The Hunkmate

The Sweetmate

The Innmate

A Man of the Month Novella

Gettin' Figgy

Mermaid For You

Pining For You

Cocky Hero Club

Arrogant Arrival (A Cocky Hero Club Novel)

Mayhem Makers

Cleric

Devour

CO-WRITTEN with ASHTON BROOKS

THE ILLICIT BROTHERHOOD

Pledge Your Loyalty

Smoke the Enemy

Crave the Illicit

Bleed for the Brotherhood

Die for the Family

This was so much fun to write! I hope you had a laugh with all Thanasis and Rose's shenanigans. Remember Alexi? The Giannis' youngest and wild son. Briefly mentioned, but he appears in Mermaid for You, and has his own story in Pining For You.

I have to think my dear friend Katie Rae for introducing me to this world! I also want to especially thank the lovely Kara Kendrick for allowing me to be a part of Candy Cane Keys! I've been extremely blessed to find so many wonderful author and reader friends through the book community. I'm beyond grateful.

Thank you to my hype team and my EPIC amazing reader group, Gail's Book Belles! Carolina, Lori, Christine, Stephanie, and Kelly – I'd be lost without you ladies! I love y'all!!!

My saint of a husband, Boo. My wonderful daughters who are so encouraging and always make me feel like I can do anything!

Most of all, thank YOU!
xoxo

About the Author

Murder. Laughter. Happily Ever After.

Gail Haris loves blending romance out of life's everyday chaos. Stories filled with humor, steam, and moments of sweetness, along with suspense and twists.

Using coffee and her imagination, Gail writes in a variety of genres, including romantic comedy, romantic suspense, and new adult/coming of age romance.

Mother of two gorgeous and hilarious girls. Other half to the Boo. Always laughing too loud and thriving on awkward situations, Gail enjoys traveling, binging series, and trying out new recipe (that sounds better than just eating).

Never stop believing in love, dreams, and yourself. And coffee…especially the coffee. Don't give up on coffee and books.

Learn more at gailharis.com

Wanna be pen pals? Subscribe for Gail Mail! Don't miss out on release announcements, exclusive giveaways, behind-the-scenes snippets, and glimpses into the chaos of her life, and more.

Sign up at https://gailharis.com/newsletter/

Let's make it awkward! Become a Book Belle!

Join Gail's reader group on Facebook!

Printed in Great Britain
by Amazon